Dinah Forever

Losers, Inc.

Standing Up to Mr. O.

You're a Brave Man, Julius Zimmerman

Lizzie at Last

7 × 9 = Trouble!

Alex Ryan, Stop That!

Perfectly Chelsea

Makeovers by Marcia

Trading Places

Being Teddy Roosevelt

The Totally Made-up Civil War Diary of Amanda MacLeish

How Oliver Olson Changed the World

One Square Inch

Fractions = Trouble!

CLAUDIA MILLS

Fractions = Trouble!

Pictures by
G. BRIAN KARAS

FARRAR STRAUS GIROUX · NEW YORK

Distributed in Canada by D&M Publishers, Inc.
Printed in May 2011 in the United States of America by RR Donnelley
& Sons Company, Harrisonburg, Virginia
First edition, 2011
1 3 5 7 9 10 8 6 4 2

mackids.com

Library of Congress Cataloging-in-Publication Data
Mills, Claudia.
    Fractions = trouble! / Claudia Mills ; pictures by G. Brian Karas. —
1st ed.
        p.   cm.
    Sequel to: 7 × 9 = trouble!
    Summary: While trying to decide on a science fair project, third-grader
Wilson struggles with fractions and, much to his embarrassment, his
parents sign him up to work with a math tutor.
    ISBN: 978-0-374-36716-9
    [1. Fractions—Fiction.   2. Science projects—Fiction.   3. Schools—
Fiction.]   I. Karas, G. Brian, ill.   II. Title.   III. Title: Fractions equal
trouble!

PZ7.M63963Fr 2011
[Fic]—dc22

                                                            2010008395

For Carol Lynch Williams

Fractions = Trouble!

1

Whenever Wilson Williams had a problem, he talked to his hamster, Pip. He had had Pip for only two weeks, but already she understood him better than anybody else in his family did.

"Multiplication was hard enough," Wilson told Pip on the first Saturday morning in April. "But now we have to do fractions."

Pip twitched her nose.

"Even worse, Mrs. Porter is giving us a huge test in three weeks."

Pip blinked.

"But that's not the worst thing."

Pip scampered across Wilson's bedspread. Luckily Wilson had his bedroom door closed so that she couldn't escape and get lost.

"Wait," Wilson said to Pip. "Don't you want to know what the worst thing is?"

He scooped up Pip and held her in both hands, facing him, as he leaned back against his pillow. Her bright little eyes really did look interested.

When Wilson had gotten Pip, her name had been Snuggles, but he had changed it to Pip, short for Pipsqueak. Pip's brother, Squiggles, was the classroom pet in Wilson's third-grade classroom.

"The worst thing," Wilson said, "is that my parents are getting me a math tutor."

Pip's eyes widened with indignation.

"I know." Wilson set her down on his knee. Instead of scurrying away, she sat very still, gazing up at him sadly. But no amount of hamster sympathy could change that one terrible fact.

A math tutor! That meant Wilson would go to school and do fractions, and then after school he'd go see Mrs. Tucker and do more fractions. He'd have fractions homework for Mrs. Porter and more fractions homework for Mrs. Tucker.

And suppose his friends at school found out. Nobody else he knew had a math tutor. There were other kids who were bad at math. There were other kids who thought fractions were hard. There even other kids who thought fractions were impossible. But Wilson had never heard of any other kid who had a math tutor.

Wilson picked up Pip again and stroked the soft fur on the top of her little head. Pip was the only good thing left in Wilson's life. From now on, the rest of his life was going to be nothing but fractions.

"Now, come on," Wilson's father said at lunch. "Cheer up. The point of a math tutor is to help you."

"You've been struggling so much," his mother went on. "First with multiplication, and now with fractions. A math tutor will make math come more easily to you."

Wilson's little brother, Kipper, who was in kindergarten, spoke up next. "Can I have a math tutor, too? Wilson and I can share the math tutor. Like we share Pip."

Wilson stopped glaring at his parents and started glaring at Kipper instead. It was annoying enough to have a little brother, but Wilson had to have a little brother who happened to love math, and who was good at it, too.

To the left of Kipper's plate sat his beanbag penguin, Peck-Peck. To the right sat his beanbag alligator, Snappy.

"What's a math tutor?" Kipper made Peck-Peck ask in a deep, growly voice. For some strange reason, Kipper seemed to think that was how a penguin should talk.

"Does a math tutor toot on a horn?" Kipper made Snappy ask. "Toot! Toot!" Snappy's head bobbed up and down with each cheerful toot, as if he were an alligator tugboat.

"Mom!" Wilson complained. "Make Kipper stop!"

But instead of giving a warning look to Kipper, she gave one to Wilson. "Kipper's

just playing." Then she actually leaned across the table and spoke directly to Snappy. "No, Snappy, a math tutor doesn't go 'Toot.' A math tutor helps people learn math. A math tutor has a very important job."

This was too much. Who else lived in a family where adults had serious conversations with beanbag alligators?

"Toot! Toot!" Snappy said again, apparently not even listening to the answer to his own stupid question.

"That's enough, Kipster," their father said.

Wilson was grateful to him for trying, but it was already too late.

"May I be excused?" Wilson asked.

"You haven't finished your grilled-cheese sandwich," his mother said.

"I'm not hungry." *Anymore*, Wilson added to himself.

Before Peck-Peck or Snappy could make any further brilliant remarks, Wilson pushed his chair back from the table and fled to his room to have an intelligent conversation with Pip.

Wilson's best friend, Josh Hernandez, came over at two. As if Wilson's mother was sorry for not standing up for him at lunch, she took Kipper for a long bike ride so that the two older boys could play undisturbed.

Wilson didn't have a video game system, and he wasn't allowed to watch TV on playdates, so he and Josh tried to build the world's fastest race car with some junk in the garage. His dad made microwave popcorn, and Wilson and Josh had a contest for throwing popcorn up into the air and catching it in their mouths. Wilson won, with seven straight mouth catches to Josh's four. He began to feel more hopeful about his life.

"Do you have an idea for your science fair project yet?" Josh asked, after missing another popcorn catch. April was science fair month at Hill Elementary.

"Nope." Wilson had been too busy trying to talk his parents out of making him have a math tutor. "Do you?"

"Uh-huh."

Wilson could tell Josh was waiting for him to ask what it was. "What is it?"

"I have to warn you," Josh said. "It's not just a good idea, it's a great idea. Are you ready?"

Wilson nodded. He couldn't believe Josh thought his idea was so wonderful. Usually Josh thought everything was terrible.

"All right. Here it is. At what temperature does a pickle explode?"

Okay, Wilson had to admit, Josh's idea was wonderful.

"You could do something about popcorn," Josh offered. "Who is better at catching popcorn in their mouths, boys or girls? Or kids or grownups? Or dogs or cats? Or kids or dogs? Or—"

Wilson shoved him good-naturedly. "I get the idea."

"You could even thrill Mrs. Porter and use fractions," Josh suggested. "Like: cats catch half as much popcorn as dogs. Or grownups catch half as much popcorn as kids. Or—"

This time Wilson shoved Josh harder. It was fine for Josh to joke about fractions. Josh was pretty good at math.

Of course, to be fair to Josh, Josh didn't

know that Wilson was about to become the only kid in the history of Hill Elementary to have a math tutor.

Wilson was going to make sure that Josh never found out.

2

At school on Monday, Wilson hung his jacket and backpack on the coatrack and then went to say hi to Squiggles. Squiggles went home with a different student every weekend. Last weekend Squiggles had visited Laura Vicks, the smartest kid in the class. Laura could *be* a math tutor.

"I hope you've all been thinking of ideas for your science fair projects!" Mrs. Porter said to the class.

Wilson had noticed how often teachers' sentences ended with exclamation marks. He wondered if Mrs. Porter really felt constantly enthusiastic about Colorado history, science fair projects, and fractions, or if she was pretending, the way his parents had pretended that having a math tutor was wonderful! Not embarrassing at all!

"Is anyone ready to share his or her science fair question with the class? Remember, a science fair project begins with a *question* that you want to answer."

Josh's hand was the first in the air, even before Laura's. Mrs. Porter looked surprised. "Josh?"

Josh waited for a long moment, and then cleared his throat to speak. "My question is: at what temperature does a pickle explode?"

Wilson could tell that Josh half expected

the class to break into thunderous applause. The kids whose faces Wilson could see clearly looked impressed.

Mrs. Porter's face showed no expression. "How do you plan to go about answering your question, Josh? What will be your *procedure*?"

"I think I'll put my pickle in the oven. I'll check it at three hundred degrees, then at four hundred degrees, and then at five hundred degrees, and keep going until it explodes."

"And what is your *hypothesis*? What is your *educated guess* about what you think is going to happen?"

"My hypothesis is that when it explodes it will make a big mess."

The class laughed.

Mrs. Porter smiled, but it was more of a worried smile than a happy smile. "Now, class, we need to talk about the importance of safety as you work on your science fair projects. Josh, have you talked to your parents yet about your idea?"

Josh nodded.

"And what did they say about it?"

"They said I should get a different idea."

The class laughed again. Mrs. Porter's smile looked relieved this time. Only Wilson heard Josh whisper, "But I'm not going to."

"Who else has an idea to share?"

Hands shot up. One kid wanted to see how long people could go without blinking. Another kid wanted to drop pieces of toast to see if toast really did always land butter-side down. Laura's friend Becca Landry was going to bake cookies and leave out different ingredients to see which ingredient was the most important. Laura was going to do something complicated with magnets and batteries. If any other kid had offered that idea, Wilson would have known that the kid's parents had thought it up. But Laura was as good in science as she was in math. She could be a science tutor as well as a math tutor.

Math tutor. Wilson had almost forgotten. He slumped down in his chair. He was supposed to have his first tutoring session with Mrs. Tucker after school on Wednesday. Instead of doing cool things like going to Josh's house to play video games or make a pickle explode, Wilson would be going to some strange lady's house to spend an hour chatting with her about fractions.

"So many wonderful ideas!" Mrs. Porter said. "Now get out your math books. It's time for math."

Time for fractions.

Wilson meant to pay attention during

math. If he could only learn how to do fractions by three o'clock on Wednesday afternoon, he could tell his parents, "Guess what? I can do fractions now!" Then they could call Mrs. Tucker and cancel the appointment. But he kept drawing pictures on his math worksheet instead: pictures of Pip, pictures of Squiggles, pictures of falling toast, pictures of puffed-up pickles ready to pop.

Maybe he would show the pictures to his parents. They would exchange glances, and then his mother would say, "Wilson is so talented at drawing. I don't think someone who is going to grow up to be an artist needs to learn how to do fractions, do you, dear?" And his father would agree. After all, Michelangelo had been a very great artist. Wilson had never heard that Michelangelo was good at fractions.

Mrs. Porter was saying something about numerators and denominators. One of them was the number on top of the little line in a fraction, and one of them was the number on the bottom. Why not just say *top* and *bottom*?

"If the numerators of two fractions are the same, the fraction with the *smaller* denominator is the *larger* fraction," Mrs. Porter said.

Wilson drew Pip eating a piece of toast. He drew Squiggles eating a pickle.

"So which fraction is larger?" Mrs. Porter asked. "One-fifth or one-eighth? Let me hear from some of you quieter students. Wilson?"

Uh-oh. The answer had something to do with the numerator and the denominator, with the top and the bottom. But which was which?

Eight was bigger than five. That much Wilson knew.

"One-eighth?" he guessed.

"No," Mrs. Porter said. She explained it again, but Wilson still didn't understand. She could explain it a thousand times, and Wilson still wouldn't understand.

Wilson had a better idea than Josh's for a science fair project: what was the best way to make a math book explode?

After school Wilson met Kipper outside the kindergarten room so they could walk home together.

"Guess what?" Kipper shouted as soon as he saw Wilson.

Wilson shrugged. He wasn't in the mood for guessing, especially if the guess had anything to do with Peck-Peck and Snappy, each clutched in one of Kipper's hands.

"You know how you and Josh were

talking about the science fair when Mom and I got home from our bike ride on Saturday?"

"Yeah. What about it?"

"My class is going to do the science fair, too!"

"So?"

"So *I'm* going to have a science fair project! With one of those big white boards that folds up, with pictures and words all over it! Our parents can help with the writing part, Mrs. Macky said. Brothers and sisters can help. *You* can help!"

Hooray, Wilson thought glumly.

"And—what's the long, hard word that starts with *H*? *Hippopotamus*?"

"*Hypothesis*."

"I'm going to have a hypothesis!"

Wilson gave in and returned Kipper's huge grin. It was great, in a way, how little

kids could still be so excited about everything. And no little kid was ever more excited than Kipper.

Wilson felt a lot less like grinning on
Wednesday afternoon when he and his
mother, Kipper, Peck-Peck, and Snappy set
out to walk to Mrs. Tucker's house for his
first day of math tutoring.

"You don't have to walk with me," Wilson
objected. "It's only a few blocks."

"I want to go with you today," his mother
said. "At least for your first session. To make
sure you find Mrs. Tucker's house and to
introduce you to each other."

Wilson sighed. He didn't mind so much
that his mother was coming with him; he
minded that Kipper was coming with him—
Kipper *and* Snappy *and* Peck-Peck. But of
course Kipper was too young to be left at

home alone. Instead, Kipper would show off, and make Snappy and Peck-Peck talk about fractions, and Mrs. Tucker would think how cute Kipper was, and how smart. And how un-cute Wilson was, and how dumb.

Luckily, when they reached Mrs. Tucker's house—a yellow house with bright blue shutters and hundreds of daffodils in bloom—Wilson's mother told Kipper to wait quietly.

"I want to talk to the math tutor!" Kipper whined.

Their mother silenced Kipper with a glance.

Wilson wasn't sure what a math tutor would look like. When she opened the door, Mrs. Tucker turned out to be a small, birdlike woman, hardly taller than Wilson. She was as colorful as her house,

wearing a long purple skirt, a yellow sweater, and red and blue glass beads. At least she wasn't wearing earrings shaped like numbers, or a sweatshirt with equations on it.

Wilson's mother presented him to Mrs. Tucker, handed her a check, gave Wilson a quick hug, and left with Kipper.

Wilson wished he could go with them.

"Come on in!" Mrs. Tucker said.

Wilson did.

Mrs. Tucker led Wilson to a room off her kitchen. In it was a table and chairs, like the table and chairs in Wilson's classroom. A low bookshelf held lots of books, probably all boring books about math. But then Wilson recognized a couple of the titles: *Charlotte's Web* and one of the Harry Potter books.

"So," Mrs. Tucker said, once Wilson was

seated at the table. "Your mother said you need some help with fractions."

"I guess so." He needed help eliminating fractions from the planet.

The thought made him smile, and Mrs. Tucker said, "What?"

"Nothing."

"Come on, tell me. You just thought of something funny. If we're going to be spending two hours a week together, we might as well share anything funny."

Two hours a week? Wilson had thought he was coming *once* a week. But so far Mrs. Tucker was nice, so he told her about eliminating fractions from the planet.

She laughed. "All right. Poof! All fractions are gone! If you ruled the world, what would there be instead of fractions?"

"Drawing. And hamsters."

"Do you have a hamster?"

Wilson told her about Pip and Squiggles.

"Great! Once I had two hamsters, named Twitchell and Boo-Boo."

Mrs. Tucker pulled out a large sheet of paper and three tubs, one of markers, one of crayons, and one of colored pencils.

"Draw me some hamsters," she said. "Draw me four hamsters."

Wilson stared at her. He knew his mother wasn't paying Mrs. Tucker so that he could sit at Mrs. Tucker's house drawing hamsters. He could sit drawing hamsters at home for free. But he wasn't about to complain and beg to do fractions instead.

And pretty soon he was doing fractions, sort of.

Pip was ¼ of the group of four hamsters.

Squiggles and Pip together were ¾ of the group of four hamsters.

Twitchell was ¼ of the group.

Twitchell and Boo-Boo together were ¾ of the group.

When the hour was over, Wilson had filled four large sheets of paper with hamster drawings, and Mrs. Tucker had never once used the words *numerator* or *denominator*.

Wilson had to admit it hadn't been as bad as he had thought it would be. But *numerator* and *denominator* had to be coming. Mrs. Porter's test wasn't going to be a hamster-drawing test, where kids passed if they could draw ten hamsters in fifteen minutes. At school they were even starting to add fractions together. With Wilson's luck, soon they'd be subtracting fractions, and multiplying fractions, and dividing fractions. Wilson would still be the only kid who couldn't do it, however many hamsters he drew.

"Do you want to take your pictures

home, or may I keep them?" Mrs. Tucker asked as Wilson stood up to leave.

Wilson hesitated. It would be cool to have the pictures for his room. But Laura and Becca both lived nearby. Wilson imagined seeing them on their bikes—kids who didn't go to math tutors had time to ride bikes after school. They would see his rolled-up sheets of paper, and one of them would say, "What are those, Wilson?" And he'd say, "Oh, those are the hamsters I drew with my math tutor." And they'd say, "What? You have a math tutor?"

Wilson shook his head.

"You can keep them," he said.

4

How did it go?" Wilson's mother asked when he walked in the door.

"Okay." He wasn't going to tell her that he had spent the whole time drawing hamsters. She might fire Mrs. Tucker and get him a different math tutor who would make him spend the whole time doing math.

Fortunately, his mom didn't ask anything else, though Wilson could tell she wanted to. He hated seeing the hopeful look on her face, as if one hour with a math tutor would have solved her son's problems with fractions forever.

"She said I'm going to be seeing her *two* hours a week," Wilson said. "I thought I only had to go *one* hour a week."

"No, it's going to be twice a week, on Wednesday afternoon and Saturday morning. We're lucky that Mrs. Tucker had these openings in her schedule."

Lucky wasn't the word Wilson would have chosen.

Pip wasn't in her cage in Wilson's room. He found her in Kipper's room. Or rather, he found her inside the tent in Kipper's room.

Since their overnight family camping trip one weekend during spring break, Kipper had been sleeping every night in the small tent he had begged his parents to set up in his bedroom. Wilson couldn't decide if the tent was cool, or stupid. Maybe cool in a stupid sort of way. Or stupid in a cool sort of way.

Inside the tent Kipper was reading a story to Pip, Peck-Peck, and Snappy. The only problem was that Kipper couldn't read. So he was holding the book and making up his own story, about three friends named Pip, Peck-Peck, and Snappy.

Wilson crawled inside the tent and picked up Pip, who had been dozing in a tightly curled little ball.

"And they lived happily ever after," Kipper finished quickly. "What is your science fair project going to be?" he asked Wilson.

"I don't know." Josh's popcorn-catching idea was funny, but Wilson didn't feel like finding a whole bunch of kids and

grownups and dogs and cats who were willing to let him test how many kernels of popcorn they could catch in their mouths. He doubted that even his own parents would agree to do it.

He stroked Pip's firm little body, feeling the gentle rise and fall of her breathing. Maybe he could time how many hours a day she slept versus how many hours a day she ran in her wheel. Or he could teach her to do tricks, to see how smart she was. He could probably teach her to do some amazing tricks.

"Actually," Wilson said, "I'm going to do experiments with Pip."

Kipper's face lit up. "Can I do experiments with Pip, too? Pip is my hamster, too!"

"No!" Wilson hated that Pip was Kipper's hamster, too. Kipper already had Peck-Peck and Snappy. Why did he need half of a hamster? Half of *Wilson's* hamster. "Think of your own idea."

Kipper pushed out his lower lip: step one of Kipper crying.

Kipper's eyes started to water: step two of Kipper crying.

Before Kipper's mouth could start to tremble—step three of Kipper crying—Wilson said, "I'll help you think of another idea, an even better idea."

"Like what?"

Good question. Nothing was better than doing experiments with hamsters. Wilson looked around, desperate for inspiration.

"Like—something about tents."

"Like what about tents?"

At least Kipper's mouth wasn't trembling and his eyes had stopped watering. His lip still stuck out, though.

"We'll ask Dad when he comes home."

Their dad loved anything to do with camping. If anyone could think of a good science fair project about tents, he would be the one.

Wilson crawled back out of the tent with Pip, soon to be co-winner of the Nobel Prize in Science Fairs.

"Tents," their father said as he speared the first meatball on top of his spaghetti.

"We could set up all our tents"—their family owned three—"and see which tent is the biggest," Kipper suggested.

That didn't seem, to Wilson, like the right kind of question for a science fair project. Which person in their family was the tallest? Their dad. Which person was the shortest? Kipper. Or Pip, if she counted as a person. It was too easy. But he didn't say anything, for fear that his father would change the subject and start asking him about his math tutoring.

"Let's think a bit more," his dad said. "What do we want a tent for?"

"To keep out bears!" Kipper made Peck-Peck and Snappy jerk their heads with fear of bears. Peck-Peck and Snappy sat at the table every night for dinner, while Pip ate alone in her cage. It was another thing in Wilson's life that wasn't fair.

"Well, a tent won't provide much protection from bears. But it definitely helps with rain and wind. All three of our tents are waterproof, but I know from experience that some tents do better in the wind than others, depending on their size and shape. We have one big, tall tent, and one small, low tent—that's the one in your room, Kipper—and a medium-sized one. How about setting up all three tents outside in the backyard on a windy night and seeing which one holds up best in the wind?"

"I think the big one will be the best," Kipper said.

Their father looked as if he thought that was the wrong answer, but didn't want to come right out and say it. "Okay, boys—Wilson, you can help with this, too. Think about a sailboat. Which sail would catch more wind: a big, tall one or a little, low one?"

"The big one," Wilson said. That seemed obvious.

"Yes," their dad said. "But when it comes to tents, you *don't* want them to catch the wind, right? So that means that, in the wind—"

"A little one would be better," Wilson said, since Kipper had obviously stopped listening to their dad's explanation.

Kipper's face lit up with a new idea. "Can

we put Peck-Peck and Snappy in the tents when we test them?"

"I don't see why not," their dad said. "And then we can find out whether a small, low tent really is better for camping in the wind."

"Boys, you need to let your father eat his supper," their mother said. As if Wilson had said or done a single thing so far to distract anybody from eating anything. "Wilson, have you come up with an idea for your project?"

"I'm going to teach tricks to Pip and see how long it takes her to learn them."

"When is the science fair?" his dad asked, swallowing another meatball.

"In two and a half weeks. On a Friday." The same day as the big horrible fractions test. If only Wilson could pass that test and never have to go to a math tutor again.

"Good luck," his dad said. He made it sound as if two and a half weeks wasn't going to be enough time. Well, his dad might know a lot about tents and sailboats, but this showed how little he knew about hamsters.

"May I be excused?" Wilson asked.

"Your dad is still eating," his mother said.

"Just let him go," his dad said.

As Wilson was heading away from the table, his father called after him, "Oh, Wilson? I forgot to ask: what happened with the math tutor today?"

Wilson pretended that he hadn't heard. Off he raced to start training Pip.

Sit. Stay. Roll over. Shake paws. Those were the tricks people taught their dogs. Wilson decided to start with shaking paws.

He took Pip out of her cage and placed her on his bed.

"Pip," he said. "Shake!"

Then he took her little paw and shook it.

He did it a few more times so she would get the idea and learn what the command sounded like. Each time, he said it slowly and clearly: "Sh-ake!"

He knew he was forgetting something. Oh, he needed to have treats, to reward her whenever she did it right.

Into her cage Pip went. Wilson ran down to the kitchen, grabbed a plastic bag of baby carrots, and ran back.

This time he offered Pip a nibble of a carrot right after he shook her paw.

"Shake!"

He shook her paw.

He gave her a nibble of carrot.

"Shake!"

He shook her paw again and gave her another nibble of carrot.

But Pip never offered him her paw, and that was what the trick was all about. The trick wasn't shaking hands with a hamster. The trick was getting the hamster to shake hands with you.

"Shake!"

Pip darted across Wilson's bed.

"Shake!" Wilson shouted after her.

Maybe two and a half weeks wasn't going to be enough time, after all—either to train Pip or to learn fractions. Two and a half *years* wouldn't be enough time to learn fractions.

At Josh's house, after school on Thursday, Josh and Wilson selected the largest pickle from the jar of kosher dill pickles that Josh had made his mother buy. This was the pickle that was about to meet its doom.

"I still don't think this is a good idea," Josh's mother said.

"That's what Einstein's mother said," Josh told her. "Right before he discovered . . . What did Einstein discover?"

"The theory of relativity," Josh's mother answered automatically, as she gazed down at the pickle.

"Well," Josh said, "your son is about to discover the theory of explosivity."

Josh's father appeared in the doorway. Both of Josh's parents worked at home, doing something on their computers.

"Ramon, what if it does explode?" Josh's mother asked Josh's father.

"Well, it's just a pickle," Josh's father said. "I don't think it will make a very big explosion."

"The atom bomb was just an atom!" Josh's mom shot back. "And it made a very big explosion!"

Wilson was surprised that even as they kept telling Josh what a bad idea this was, they didn't tell him not to do it. His parents would have said, "No exploding pickles!" just as they said, "No video games! No TV on playdates! No fighting with Kipper!"

"Are you ready?" Josh asked his pickle.

The pickle didn't answer.

Josh apparently took that as a yes.

He put the pickle in a pan and slid the pan into the oven. Then he set the temperature to 350 degrees. That was the temperature for baking cookies, Josh had told Wilson. Since cookies didn't explode, that would be the temperature to start with.

Luckily, Josh's oven had a glass window in the door. Josh and Wilson pulled up two kitchen chairs and sat down in front of the oven to watch. His parents watched for a while, too, and then they drifted away.

When fifteen minutes had gone by, and the pickle hadn't exploded at 350 degrees, Josh turned up the oven to 400 degrees. He wrote down the temperatures and times in his science fair notebook.

Wilson saw Josh's title on the cover of

the book: "At what temperchur does a pickel explod?" Josh was as bad at spelling as Wilson was at math.

When the pickle didn't explode at 400 degrees, Josh turned the oven up to 425, and then to 450, and 500, and 550. Through the glass, the pickle was starting to look shriveled and shrunken in the middle, with brown patches all over it, as if it had a skin disease. But it still didn't look close to exploding.

"Maybe we should go play some video games in the basement," Josh suggested. "If the pickle explodes, we'll hear it."

"I think we should stay here," Wilson said. "Besides, don't you think the pickle is starting to smell? Like it's burning, or something?"

The boys peered more closely at the pickle through the glass window. It was definitely turning black. Smoke was pouring out from it, too.

Josh's mother ran into the kitchen, his father close behind her. The next thing Wilson knew, the oven had been turned off, the charred body of the pickle was in the sink under cold running water, and all the kitchen windows had been flung open to get rid of the smoke before the smoke alarm could go off.

"You could have set the house on fire!" Josh's mother said.

"That's what Einstein's mother said, too," Josh said.

After his parents returned to their computers, Josh rescued the pickle from the sink. It was amazingly lightweight, a black pickle skeleton. He took a picture of it with his dad's digital camera.

"To put up on my science fair board," he

told Wilson. "I'll bring in the actual pickle, too. As evidence."

"So I guess pickles don't explode," Wilson said.

"Pickles don't explode in the oven," Josh corrected him. "I'm going to give my parents a couple of days to get over this, and then I'll try it again in the microwave. Can you come over on Saturday morning?"

"Sure." Then Wilson remembered. He had to go see Mrs. Tucker on Saturday morning. "I mean, no. I have something else I have to do."

Josh looked suspicious. Wilson knew Josh knew that he didn't take piano lessons or play a spring sport, and he wouldn't have a dentist appointment on the weekend.

"What are you doing on Saturday?" Josh asked.

Wilson couldn't tell him.

"Just stuff." Wilson gazed down at his feet. "Just some stuff my parents are making me do."

Now Josh looked hurt.

"Okay," Josh said stiffly, as he patted his burned, soaked pickle dry with a paper towel. "I guess I'll have to explode my pickle without you."

6

By Saturday, Pip still hadn't learned how to shake paws or roll over.

At ten o'clock on Saturday morning, just as Josh's pickle was probably exploding in the microwave, Wilson presented himself at Mrs. Tucker's door. At least this time his mother and Kipper had stayed home to work on Kipper's science fair project, busy setting up all three tents in the backyard; the weather forecast was for a windy night.

Wilson had wondered if Mrs. Tucker would ask him to draw hamsters again, and she did!

This time he drew a group of eight hamsters and a group of two hamsters. He could see that in the group of eight hamsters, one little hamster wasn't a very big part of the group. That was why ⅛ wasn't a very big fraction. But in the group of two hamsters, one hamster was half of the whole group. That was why ½ was a bigger fraction than ⅛ even though 8 was a bigger number than 2.

The bottom number in the fraction was for the size of the whole group—how many total hamsters. The top number told how many members, or parts, of the group you were talking about.

"Which one is the numerator?" Wilson asked.

"The numerator is the top," Mrs. Tucker said. "The denominator is the bottom. Some people remember it this way. Since the numerator is on top of the denominator, this means that *N* for numerator comes before *D* for denominator. So you think of the words *Nice Dog*."

"I wish it was *Nice Hamster*," Wilson said.

"Well, that could still be a good way to remember it, because *nice* comes first either way, and *nice* stands for *numerator*."

"I'm going to think that the Nice Numerator is on top, and the Dumb Denominator is on the bottom."

"Wilson, that's wonderful!" Mrs. Tucker said.

As he was getting ready to go home, Wilson told Mrs. Tucker about the science fair. Pip was Nice, of course, but when it came to learning tricks, she was Dumb.

"What if instead of trying to teach her to do something, you just observed what she was doing naturally?" Mrs. Tucker suggested. "You could bring Squiggles home from school for the weekend and study both hamsters together. Try to find out what hamsters like and dislike. Are they affected by color? By sound?"

Wilson was impressed. "Do you tutor science, too?"

Mrs. Tucker laughed. "I tutor everything. The student who comes before you on Saturdays is coming for a few weeks for help with the science fair; the student who comes after you comes for help with writing. Just the way you like to watch Pip, I like watching the different ways that kids learn."

Wilson felt better as he walked home. During his tutoring time he hadn't heard any deafening explosions anywhere. Maybe he hadn't missed out on Josh's exploding pickle, after all.

When Wilson got home, the backyard looked like a campground. Three tents were lined up in a row: the big, tall, family-sized tent; the medium-sized tent; and the small, low-to-the-ground tent moved from Kipper's bedroom. Wilson's mother was trying to explain to Kipper why he couldn't sleep in the tent now that it was set up outside.

"Tents are supposed to be outside!" Kipper said.

"At night little boys are supposed to be inside," their mother said.

"But I have it all planned out. Snappy is going to sleep in the big tent, and Peck-Peck is going to sleep in the medium-sized tent, and Pip and I are going to sleep in the little tent."

"Pip isn't sleeping in a tent!" Wilson interrupted.

"Pip isn't sleeping in a tent," his mother agreed. "Pets like what is safe and familiar."

Kipper pushed out his lower lip.

"Don't start that, Kipper," his mother said. "Snappy may sleep in a tent. Peck-Peck may sleep in a tent. Pip is sleeping in her cage. You are sleeping in your bed."

Then she turned to Wilson. "How was your time with Mrs. Tucker?"

"Okay."

His mother had that hopeful look on her face again. "Do you think she's helping you start to understand fractions any better?"

Wilson shrugged. Mrs. Tucker *was* helping him. Now he knew that the nice numerator was on top and the dumb denominator was on the bottom. And the big tent was ⅓ of the tents, while Snappy was ½ of Kipper's beanbag animals. And ½ was actually bigger than ⅓, even though 2 was a smaller number than 3. But he didn't want to say any of this to his mom. What if she made him go see Mrs. Tucker three times a week?

That afternoon Kipper and his mom made sleeping bags for Peck-Peck and Snappy out of squares of felt. They folded the squares in half (fractions!) and then sewed up two of the open sides. Peck-Peck and Snappy got new pillows, too, also made of folded felt, stuffed with cotton balls. To cut out the pillows, Kipper's mom folded each square of felt in fourths (more fractions).

"You don't take pillows on a camping trip," their dad scoffed. "On a camping trip you're supposed to rough it."

Kipper ignored this remark.

Wilson had to admit that Peck–Peck and Snappy looked cute tucked into their matching sleeping bags with their little heads resting on their matching pillows. He almost made a sleeping bag himself for Pip, but she already had a cozy hamster "cave" just her size for sleeping.

At bedtime Kipper carried the two tiny sleeping bags outside and placed them tenderly in the tents, even though the wind was dying down. So ⅔ of the tents were now occupied.

"I want to sleep in a tent," Kipper begged one last time.

His mother refused to give in.

"You belong in your bed," she repeated. "And you belong in it now."

Wilson had hoped that Josh would call and tell him what had happened with the pickle in the microwave, but he hadn't. Maybe Josh was still mad that Wilson had done his "stuff" instead, and hadn't even told him what the "stuff" was.

Finally, just before his bedtime, he called Josh. He had to call him, anyway. It was Josh's weekend for Squiggles, and Wilson needed to ask Josh if he could borrow Squiggles on Sunday to work on the science fair.

"So?" Wilson asked, as soon as Josh picked up the phone. "What happened with the pickle? Did it explode this time?"

"Nah. This pickle got all wrinkled and weird-looking, and kind of brown and bumpy, but it didn't blow up."

"So pickles don't explode."

"Pickles don't explode in an oven, or in a microwave. Next I'm going to try *boiling* one."

Wilson waited to see if Josh would invite

him to watch the third—and final?—attempt at a pickle explosion.

There was an awkward silence.

"What about you?" Josh asked. "Did you have fun doing your stuff this morning?"

"Not really," Wilson said. "Oh, can I borrow Squiggles for a while tomorrow? I've decided I'm going to make my science fair project about seeing which color hamsters like best, and it would be better to do it with two hamsters instead of just one."

"Sure," Josh said. He didn't offer to come over to help with the testing.

Then, "Well, see ya," Josh said.

"See ya," Wilson replied.

It didn't turn out to be very windy that night, after all. All three tents were fine—⅔—when Kipper went out in the morning to wake up Peck-Peck and Snappy and bring them indoors for breakfast.

Josh's dad dropped off Squiggles's cage, with Squiggles inside it, at Wilson's house mid-morning. Wilson had wondered if Pip and Squiggles would be happy to see each other, since they were sister and brother.

When he placed them both on his bed, Pip just sat there blinking, but Squiggles darted down the covers and across the room, as if to get as far away from his sister as possible. Wilson liked Kipper more than that.

"I'm going to try to find out which color hamsters like best," Wilson told Kipper, who had come into his room to help with the experiment.

"My favorite color is blue," Kipper said. "Snappy's favorite color is green. Peck-Peck's favorite color is black."

"I have a red bowl, a green bowl, a blue bowl, and a yellow bowl," Wilson continued. "I'm going to put the same amount of food in each bowl and see which color they pick."

"You don't have a black bowl," Kipper said.

"So?"

"So what if their favorite color is black, like Peck-Peck's?"

Wilson took a deep breath. "I can't try every single color in the whole world. Besides, we don't have a black bowl. The set Mom bought just has these four colors."

"What if each hamster has a different favorite color?" Kipper asked. "People don't all have the same favorite color."

Wilson did his best to remain patient. "That's what we're going to find out, Kipper."

What Wilson found out, however, was that hamsters didn't seem to have a favorite color at all. Sometimes Squiggles ran to the blue bowl, sometimes to the red one, sometimes to the green or yellow one. The same was true of Pip. Wilson wrote it all down in his science notebook, but he could tell he was getting nowhere. It had been, as far as Wilson could tell, a completely wasted hour.

"My teacher said hamsters are color-blind," Kipper suddenly said. "She says hamsters can't see color."

Wilson stared at Kipper in disbelief. *Now* was the time that Kipper shared this tidbit of information?

"Why didn't you say something sooner?" Wilson shouted.

Kipper pushed out his lower lip. "I just remembered. I can't remember *everything*, Wilson!"

Without a word, Wilson put Squiggles in his cage and Pip in her cage. He walked out of his room and slammed the door.

Wilson didn't like Kipper any better than Squiggles liked Pip, after all.

*   *   *

At school on Monday morning, Josh came up behind Wilson as Wilson carried Squiggles's cage to its corner; Squiggles had spent the night with Wilson.

"How did Squiggles do?" Josh asked.

"Terrible. I tried to find out his favorite color, but guess what? Hamsters are color-blind."

Josh laughed. "I boiled a pickle for a whole hour and it didn't explode."

Wilson laughed, too, glad Josh was being friendly again.

"Are there any other ways you can try to make a pickle explode?" Wilson asked. "You've already tried the oven, and the microwave, and boiling it."

Josh's face brightened. "Dynamite?" Then his face fell. "My parents won't let me try dynamite."

Wilson was relieved that there was at least one thing Josh's parents wouldn't let him do.

Laura, who had been standing nearby, joined the boys and clucked a friendly good morning to Squiggles in his cage. "I have an idea," Laura said.

Both boys turned toward her hopefully. Laura always had great ideas.

"I got my science fair experiment out of a book that has hundreds of science fair projects. The project it had for hamsters was testing how far hamsters can smell."

Wilson liked the idea already. "How do you do that?"

"You have to wait until they're pretty hungry. Then you try putting their food at different distances until they pick up the smell and run over to get it."

It sounded like a brilliant idea to Wilson.

"Becca is supposed to take Squiggles home this weekend, but I bet she'd let you have her turn," Laura said.

Wilson shot her a grateful grin.

"Did the book have any science fair experiments you can do with pickles?" Josh asked.

Laura shook her head.

"I didn't think so," Josh said.

Wilson went to see Mrs. Tucker on Wednesday after school and again on Saturday morning. On Saturday, he drew a group of eight hamsters. First he colored three of the hamsters brown: $\frac{3}{8}$. Then he colored two more brown: $\frac{2}{8}$. That made five brown hamsters total, out of the group of eight: $\frac{3}{8} + \frac{2}{8} = \frac{5}{8}$!

When he filled pie-shaped circles with hamsters, two hamsters in a circle of eight took up the same amount of space as one hamster in a circle of four. So ⅔ was equal to ¼!

Wilson drew hamsters until his hamster-drawing hand was about to fall off. His drawings covered Mrs. Tucker's table.

"Thank you for letting me keep these," Mrs. Tucker said. "I can use your drawings to help other children learn about fractions. I'm going to tell Mrs. Porter about them, too. I know she's always looking for new ways to get her students interested in math, and this would be perfect, especially since all of you love little Squiggles so much."

Wilson didn't tell Mrs. Tucker that he was glad she was keeping his drawings so that no one would see him carrying them home and know that he was going to a math tutor.

Instead he told Mrs. Tucker about his

progress on the science fair. "I'm going to do my smelling experiments this afternoon. I had to wait until Pip and Squiggles were hungry."

"Call me when you get your results!" Mrs. Tucker said. "How is your brother's tent project coming along?"

"He has the tents set up in the yard, but it hasn't been windy enough yet to really test them."

"Well, here in Colorado you won't have to wait long for wind."

It was true. There had been some mornings last month when it had been so windy that Wilson took Kipper's hand on their way to school so his little brother wouldn't blow away.

"Good luck this afternoon!" Mrs. Tucker said.

*　　*　　*

Neither hamster could smell the food bowl at five feet or at four feet, but they both could smell it at three feet. Wilson had proved something! He had proved an actual scientific fact! Maybe he'd even use fractions somehow on his science fair display board.

He called Mrs. Tucker and told her his results. He called Josh and told him. He'd tell Laura on Monday at school.

Wilson and Kipper left for school early Monday morning, carrying Squiggles's cage, so Wilson could get him settled in his corner before the bell. The classroom was empty when Wilson arrived; Mrs. Porter must have been down the hall in the teachers' lounge.

Once Squiggles had everything he needed—food, water, a farewell hug—Wilson turned around and saw the bulletin board.

He couldn't believe it.

There, on the board, were four large, familiar-looking pictures of hamsters.

Wilson's pictures.

Wilson's pictures made with the math tutor.

Wilson's pictures made with the math tutor for all the world to see.

8

Wilson snatched his pictures from the bulletin board, not caring as thumbtacks scattered across the floor. He ripped them in half, and in half again, and again. Then he took the torn scraps of paper and buried them in the bottom of the classroom recycling bin.

Mrs. Porter bustled into the room.

"Wilson, did you see that I put your wonderful drawings—" She broke off mid-sentence, staring at the bare bulletin board. "Why did you take them down?"

"I made them with the math tutor. Everyone will know I made them with Mrs. Tucker."

"Oh, Wilson." Mrs. Porter put an arm around his shoulders. "I wasn't going to tell the class that you made your pictures with Mrs. Tucker. I was just going to say, 'Look at what a creative way Wilson found to show us how to do fractions.' Besides, there are lots of kids who get extra help."

Wilson knew how Kipper felt when Kipper pushed out his lower lip and it started to tremble. "No one else goes to a math tutor."

"How do you know that?"

Wilson just did.

The bell rang. Hordes of third graders came racing into the room.

"I'm sorry," Mrs. Porter said softly. "I should have asked first."

Wilson turned away so she wouldn't see the Kipperish tears in his eyes.

A moment later, Josh gave him a hard, but friendly, whack on the back. "I wrote a poem last night about pickles. To put up on my science fair board. Do you want to hear it?"

Forcing a smile, Wilson nodded.

From a crumpled piece of paper, Josh read,

"Pickles boil and pickles burn.
But about pickles I have learned,
Unlike a frog, unlike a toad,
A pickle simply won't explode."

This time Wilson's grin was real. "That's good!" He couldn't resist asking, "Do frogs and toads explode?" He also saw, looking over at Josh's paper, that Josh was still spelling *pickle* as *pickel.* And he spelled *toad* as *tode.*

Josh shrugged. "I needed something to make it rhyme."

During math time, Mrs. Porter gave the class a practice test and let them grade it themselves. Wilson got eight out of ten problems right: $^8/_{10}$, which he now knew was the same as $^4/_5$. That was definitely passing. If only he could do that well on the real test on Friday, then he could stop going to see Mrs. Tucker, and he could spend his Wednesday afternoons and Saturday mornings the way everyone else in the universe did.

The memory of his hamster drawings on the bulletin board made his cheeks burn, but at least he had gotten to the room in time to rip them down before anyone else had seen them. He noticed that Mrs. Porter had quickly covered the empty bulletin board with some perfect spelling tests. It was little comfort that one of them was his.

Out on the playground at lunch, Wilson saw Kipper playing tag with his little kindergarten friends. Kipper came running up to say hello as Wilson and Josh were hanging from the monkey bars in their favorite upside-down way.

Josh swung himself right-side up to return Kipper's greeting. "What's up, Kipper, my man?"

"It's going to be windy tonight!" Kipper informed him.

Josh looked puzzled. "Are you afraid your house will blow down?"

"For the science fair! I have to see which tent does best in the wind. Remember?"

"Sure," Josh said, but Wilson didn't think he did.

"This time Peck-Peck is going to sleep in the little, low tent. Snappy is still going to sleep in the big, tall one." Kipper held both Peck-Peck and Snappy up for Josh to see and made them do a little dance. "I don't have anyone sleeping in the middle-sized tent."

"How about a pickle?" Josh suggested. "I have a pickle that likes adventures."

"You can't put a pickle in a tent!" Kipper giggled.

"Why not? You haven't met my pickle yet."

Kipper giggled again. "When can I meet your pickle?"

"I'll bring him over for a playdate. Yeah, we'll have a playdate: you and me and Wilson and my pickle."

Wilson was getting irritated. He had no

intention of having a playdate with his little brother and Josh's pickle. First Kipper had half of Wilson's hamster; now Kipper was taking half of Wilson's best friend. One half plus one half added up to the equivalent of one whole big thing that Kipper was taking away from Wilson.

"And Snappy and Peck-Peck can play, too," Kipper added.

"Of course Snappy and Peck-Peck."

"When can you come?" Kipper asked, as if he was going to start counting the hours.

"How about Wednesday? Right after school on Wednesday?"

"No," Kipper said. "It can't be Wednesday afternoon."

"Why not?"

Before Wilson could hiss a warning to Kipper, it was too late.

"Because that's when Wilson goes to the math tutor."

"Kipper!" Wilson shouted.

Wilson didn't stick around to see if Kipper was going to start crying, as usual. He shot one quick look at Josh. Josh was staring at his feet. Wilson could tell that Josh was embarrassed. Embarrassed to be Wilson's friend.

Wilson turned around and walked across the blacktop to where some other kids were shooting hoops. He didn't look back.

9

As soon as the boys got home from school, Wilson told his mother what Kipper had said to Josh on the playground. For once, Wilson's mother wasn't mad at him, but was mad at Kipper.

His mother's face looked very serious as she sat Kipper down and said, "Kipper, Wilson can be the one to tell his friends about his math tutor, if he wants to."

"But Josh asked." Kipper's face twisted

into its most pathetic expression. "He wanted to come over on Wednesday afternoon, and I said Wednesday afternoon wasn't good, and he asked why, and so I told him."

"Having a tutor is private," their mother explained.

Wilson couldn't agree with her more. But he also knew that if having a math tutor was as wonderful as his parents claimed, it wouldn't be private. His mother was practically admitting that having a math tutor was embarrassing.

Which it was. So embarrassing that Wilson's own best friend couldn't look him in the face once he found out.

"I'm sorry, Wilson," Kipper sniffed in his most pathetic voice. "Peck-Peck and Snappy are sorry, too."

What could Wilson say? "That's okay."

Wilson's mother gave him a reassuring smile. Snappy and Peck-Peck tried to kiss him.

Wilson pushed them away.

Alone in his room, he lay on his bed for a long time, holding Pip and petting her small, soft head. Pip didn't care that Wilson went to a math tutor.

Why couldn't everybody else in the world be more like Pip?

That evening the wind rattled the windows and roared down the chimney as Kipper headed out to the backyard with Peck-Peck and Snappy to put them into their sleeping bags. Wilson was glad that Pip wasn't sleeping in the empty third tent.

"Go with Kipper, Wilson," his mother said. "It's so windy out there."

As if Wilson could do anything to make the wind stop its howling and shrieking.

First the two boys crawled into Peck-Peck's low tent, and Kipper slipped Peck-Peck into his sleeping bag. He shone the beam of his flashlight onto Peck-Peck's beak.

"Good night, Peck-Peck!"

Then the two boys unzipped the flap to Snappy's tall tent. Kipper gave Snappy a good-night kiss before tucking him into his sleeping bag.

"Snappy's afraid," Kipper said. "Snappy doesn't like the wind."

Wilson wasn't sure he liked the wind, either. The sides of the tent shook as if the Big Bad Wolf were huffing and puffing to blow the tent down. The wind definitely felt worse in Snappy's taller tent than in Peck-Peck's low-to-the-ground model.

"Snappy doesn't have to sleep here," Wilson pointed out. "He could sleep in Peck-Peck's tent with Peck-Peck." For that matter, Snappy could sleep in the house.

"He'll be okay," Kipper said, but he sounded uncertain. "You'll be okay," he told Snappy, in a more confident voice. "See you later, alligator!"

Kipper had just learned that saying. Wilson knew he thought it was funny saying it to Snappy because Snappy *was* an alligator.

The wind was so fierce all night that Wilson had trouble sleeping. He wondered if Pip was frightened, too, listening to the wind from her cage. Maybe hamsters didn't hear sounds the way people did, just as hamsters couldn't see the colors people saw. He hoped so.

Wilson dreamed that he was doing fractions. In his dream, he was taking the big fractions test, and he got all the problems wrong, and Mrs. Porter marked a huge red zero on the top of his paper, and then she thumbtacked it to the bulletin board for the whole class to see.

By morning, the wind had died down. Still in his pajamas, without waiting to put on a jacket, Kipper ran outside to rescue Peck-Peck and Snappy and bring them into the warm, snug kitchen for breakfast.

A moment later, Wilson heard Kipper's piercing wail. This wasn't Kipper's ordinary kindergarten crying. Something terrible must have happened to Kipper.

Wilson's parents raced outside, with Wilson right behind them.

Apparently unharmed, Kipper was standing with his eyes squeezed shut, sobbing as if his heart would break, as if it had already broken.

Two of the tents were there, looking none the worse for their night in the

storm. One of the tents was gone, the big, tall one, gone completely, vanished without a trace.

Snappy's tent.

And with it, Snappy.

Wilson's dad drove around the neighborhood looking for the tent while Wilson and Kipper got dressed and had breakfast, or tried to have breakfast. Kipper was crying too hard to eat.

"It can't have blown very far," Wilson's mother said, pulling Kipper onto her lap as they all sat at the kitchen table. "Daddy will be back any minute now, telling us he found it."

Wilson was the first to hear the car in the driveway; Kipper was first out the front door. But their father's face was grim with disappointment.

"I didn't see it anywhere," he confessed. "Lots of tree limbs on lawns, and even one whole tree blown down. No tent."

"We'll have to go on foot and walk through people's backyards," Wilson's mother said. "No, not now, Kipper. I'm sorry, honey, but you boys have to go to school. I'll take a long walk this morning, as soon as you leave, I promise. And if I find the tent, I'll come to school and tell both of you. So come on, honey, get Peck-Peck, and off you go."

"Peck-Peck doesn't want to go to school without Snappy!"

Wilson felt like crying himself. His mother's eyes were glistening, and his dad was suddenly very busy clearing the breakfast dishes from the table.

As the boys were getting ready to head out the front door, without any little beanbag animals, Kipper ran back and grabbed Peck-Peck. The three of them trudged off to school.

Please, please, please, please let us see the tent on the way, Wilson prayed. He'd even forgive Kipper for telling Josh about the math tutor, if only they'd find Snappy.

But they didn't.

On the Friday morning of the big math test that would decide whether Wilson was going to be free from the math tutor forever, Wilson stood in the gymnasium next to his science project board as the judges came by to ask questions. It was good to have something else to think about besides $\frac{3}{8} + \frac{4}{8} = \frac{7}{8}$.

"What made you decide to study hamsters' sense of smell?" one judge asked.

Wilson explained that he had first tried to teach his hamsters tricks and then to find out their favorite color. He could tell that the judge was impressed he had tried so many things that didn't work.

"That's what science is all about," the man said. "Sometimes we learn more from failure than we do from success."

It was an interesting thought. Maybe the judge would like Josh's project best of all: Josh had had nothing *but* failure.

Josh and his pickle had never ended up coming over for a playdate with Wilson and Kipper. Wilson couldn't tell if Josh had been avoiding him ever since Josh found out about Wilson's math tutor; maybe he, Wilson, was the one who had been avoiding Josh. Either way, they hadn't seen much of each other.

Wilson noticed that Josh had brought

his oven-baked pickle to the science fair. The poor pickle deserved that much, at least.

Kipper's board had turned out to be cute and funny, with Kipper's own drawings of the three tents and Kipper's big kindergarten printing: *The tll tnt bloo awa.* Kipper's spelling was even worse than Josh's spelling, but Josh was in third grade and Kipper was only in kindergarten.

It had been three days since the windy night, and the tent hadn't been found. Snappy hadn't been found, either. Kipper never let go of Peck-Peck now, but he had stopped making Peck-Peck talk. Without Snappy, Peck-Peck had nobody to talk to. Wilson felt a lump in his throat whenever he saw Kipper clutching his shabby, lonely little penguin.

The science fair judging lasted all

morning. Wilson hardly touched his pizza at lunch, even though pizza was his favorite, cut in eighths. He saw that Josh ate two pieces: ⅛, or ¼. Lucky Josh didn't have to worry about passing the fractions test.

Finally, after lunch, Mrs. Porter told the class to clear their desks and make sure they each had a sharpened pencil. Then she handed out the tests.

Scribbling furiously, with his pencil as sharp as sharp could be, Wilson kept his thoughts on groups of hamsters: comparing groups of hamsters, adding groups of hamsters, even subtracting groups of hamsters. No longer was he confused by nice numerators and dumb denominators. Maybe he'd let Mrs. Porter have one of his hamster drawings to put up on her bulletin board next year, when he was safely down the hall in fourth grade.

Mrs. Porter graded the tests while the class was at art, so Wilson had his to take home by the end of the day: only three problems wrong, out of twenty! He couldn't wait to show his parents. He was done with the math tutor forever! He could do his times tables! He could do fractions! What else was there left to do?

The P.A. system clicked on for the announcement of which science fair projects had been chosen to go on to the district science fair, three for each grade. The principal read the results in order, from little kids to big kids.

For kindergarten, one of the winners was "Tents" by Kipper Williams!

For third grade, one of the winners was "How Far Can a Hamster Smell?" by Wilson Williams!

Laura's batteries project won, too, of course.

Josh's pickle project did not.

Josh made his pickle pretend to cry. As the pickle continued to wail with disappointment, Wilson burst out laughing with mingled amusement and relief. Now that he wouldn't have to spend Wednesday afternoon and Saturday morning with the math tutor, he and Josh could be friends again. He wouldn't even mind if Josh was nice to Kipper sometimes. Wilson wanted to be nice to Kipper himself, he felt so sorry for his little brother.

If only the big, tall tent hadn't blown away.

If only Snappy hadn't been in the big, tall tent when it blew away.

It was wonderful waking up Saturday morning: no math tutor! Wilson almost missed Mrs. Tucker, who had been so kind and encouraging, and who had let him sit at her table drawing hundreds of hamsters. But not enough to want to go see her ever again.

At nine-thirty, when Wilson would have been dressed and ready to leave for his tutoring session, he was still lying on the couch watching cartoons with Pip and Kipper and Peck-Peck.

Wilson's mother appeared in the family room. "Wilson! What are you doing? Why aren't you dressed? You have to be at Mrs. Tucker's in half an hour!"

Wilson stared at her in disbelief. "Fractions are over! I passed the fractions test! I did great on the fractions test!"

"Because you had a math tutor," his mother said. "You're doing better in math than you ever have. Why would you stop seeing Mrs. Tucker now?"

"But—" Wilson didn't know how to finish the sentence.

Did his parents expect him to go to a math tutor for the rest of his life? Would he be ninety years old and hobbling off with his cane to see his math tutor, while all the other old people were watching cartoons and playing with their hamsters?

"Wilson," his mother said in her low warning voice. "Get. Dressed. And. Go."

America might be a free country, but Wilson's house was not a free house.

He got dressed and went. He heard his mother calling to Kipper to hurry up so they could leave on a morning bike ride around the neighborhood before it got too hot. Wilson stomped out the door without waiting.

Everybody else in the world except for

Wilson was out riding bikes, washing cars, playing ball in the street, having yard sales. Even Mrs. Tucker's next-door neighbor was having a yard sale—lots of baby stuff, racks of clothes, and camping gear spread out all over the lawn. One of the tents set up for sale looked just like their big, tall tent that had blown away. Maybe Wilson's dad would want to come over and buy it to replace the other one. But there was no replacing Snappy.

Wilson plunked himself down on Mrs. Tucker's front porch to wait for the kid before him to come out. He could hear Mrs. Tucker talking to somebody inside the house, by the front door, so he could tell they were almost finished. He was glad there was at least one other kid in the world going to a math tutor. He and the other kid could grow old together.

Mrs. Tucker's door opened, and the other kid came out.

Wilson stared at the other kid.

The other kid stared at Wilson.

It was Josh!

11

ut you're good at math!" Wilson said.

"I'm not good at spelling," Josh said. "So last weekend my parents told me I had to have a spelling tutor, starting today."

Josh gave Wilson a huge, sheepish grin. Wilson's grin was even bigger. No wonder Josh had looked so embarrassed when Kipper had spilled the secret about Wilson's tutor.

"Come on in, Wilson," Mrs. Tucker said. "I want to hear all about the fractions test and the science fair. Josh told me that congratulations are in order."

"See you later, alligator," Josh said.

Wilson felt his grin fade. He was remembering how Kipper had tucked Snappy into his little felt sleeping bag on that cold, windy night.

If only the tent next door were really their tent.

Wilson's heart clenched like a fist inside his chest.

Maybe . . .

It was worth asking.

"Can you wait one minute?" he asked Mrs. Tucker.

Without stopping to explain, he raced over to look more closely at the big, tall tent set up at the yard sale.

The tent had a little rip by the front door exactly like the little rip by the front door on Snappy's tent. It had a broken zipper pull just like the broken zipper pull on Snappy's tent.

Wilson peeked inside: there was no little alligator in a sleeping bag.

Wilson found the man in charge of the yard sale, who was sitting in a folding chair by a card table with a cash box.

"Excuse me? The big, tall tent over there? Where did you get it? It didn't blow here that night when it was so windy, did it?"

The man gave a loud belly laugh. "It sure did. There was no name on it, and no way I could find out whose tent it was. And I sure couldn't figure out why anybody would be camping on a night like that. Is it yours?"

Wilson nodded. But he didn't care about the tent. He cared about what had been inside the tent. He was almost afraid to ask his next question.

"There wasn't—there wasn't a little beanbag alligator in it, was there?"

"You bet. It's around here somewhere." A worried look creased the man's face. "Unless somebody bought it already."

Wilson's heart stopped beating.

"I put all the stuffed animals in that bin over there." The man pointed. "Go and check."

"Wilson!" It was his mom, calling over to him as she rode by on her tandem bike, with Kipper pedaling behind her. "It's past ten! Why aren't you at Mrs. Tucker's?"

Wilson didn't answer. Frantically, he dug through the bin, pushing aside a

Barbie with only one leg and a broken toy soldier.

He could hear Kipper's piercing voice: "Mom! That looks just like *our* tent!"

If someone had already bought Snappy, Wilson would die.

Kipper came running toward Wilson, as Wilson tossed aside a bear with torn overalls and a stained pink elephant.

Then Wilson saw a bit of faded green, alligator green, and then a whole little familiar alligator body.

The next thing Wilson knew, Kipper was hugging him, and his mother was hugging him, and Peck-Peck and Snappy were hugging him. He knew that if his dad and Pip had been there, they would have been hugging him, too.

Wilson had a funny thought, a thought he wanted to remember to tell his math tutor.

STUFFED TOY

A family was like fractions, really.

Kipper and his mother and his father and Pip and Snappy and Peck-Peck were the parts.

And they made Wilson's happiness whole.

A NOTE FROM THE AUTHOR

Everybody is bad at something. I have always been bad at math.

Part of the reason that I was bad at it was that I would spend my time in math class writing poems all over my math papers. That certainly didn't help. But I also never felt comfortable with numbers the way I did with words. Even worse than numbers were letters in equations like x and y. To this day I feel stressed whenever I see any equation that has x or y in it. I had an easier time mastering my times tables than Wilson does, because I have a pretty good memory and could learn them by rote. But, oh, fractions were hard!

Unlike me, my younger sister was good at math—very good at math. (Actually, she is good at almost everything.) For a while, that bothered me. But then I realized that she could help me with my math homework, and all throughout high school she did. (She was also a math tutor—as good as Mrs. Tucker—for other students at school.)

Now I am the mother of two grownup sons. One of them is a math whiz; the other one, well, he takes after me and struggles with it. For him, as for me, fractions were—and are—trouble!